The Loup Garou

The Loup

Garou

Berthe Amoss

PELICAN PUBLISHING COMPANY
GRETNA 1979

Library of Congress Cataloging in Publication Data

Amoss, Berthe.
    The Loup Garou.

    SUMMARY: In 18th-century Nova Scotia as the English
attempt to force out the French, one family draws upon
its knowledge of the legendary werewolf, loup-garou.
    1. Nova Scotia—History—1713-1763—juvenile fiction.
[1. Nova Scotia—History—1713-1763—Fiction.
2. Werewolves—Fiction. 3. Cajuns—Fiction]
I. Title.
PZ7.A5177Lo   [Fic]   79-20536
ISBN 0-88289-189-8

Manufactured in the United States of America

Published by Pelican Publishing Company, Inc.
630 Burmaster Street, Gretna, Louisiana 70053

To my family

Chapter I

If you could go back to the year 1755, to a place that was called Acadia but is now called Nova Scotia, you would see three little boys hunting in the woods. Robert, Louis, and Little Otter are hunting partridge. Robert, the smallest, has a pole with a noose on the end.

"You'll never catch him," Louis says. "You're too short."

"I may be short, but this pole is long and I know what I'm doing. Watch!" Robert creeps towards a birch tree. A partridge is perched on a low branch. Robert creeps very quietly. He raises the pole very carefully. Just as Robert is about to pass the noose over the partridge's head, Louis sneezes and the bird flies away. Robert looks at Louis.

"I can't help it if I have to sneeze!"

"I will get our dinner," says Little Otter,
bending his bow until the ends almost meet.
"We Micmacs make our bows of fir and my

arrows are very straight." He touches the wood-
pecker feathers in the shaft. "I will get a rabbit
for dinner."

"Not if Louis sneezes," says Robert.

"And not if you talk," says Louis. "You will
scare everything away."

"Not everything—you can't scare the Loup
Garou* away!" says Robert.

"What is the Loup Garou?"

"I think it is a wolf, isn't it Robert?"

"It is worse than a wolf," answers Robert. "It
is a man who changes into a wolf at twilight!
Last night when we told stories after supper
my mother told about the Loup Garou. She
said there was one on the ship with her grand-
father when he came from France long ago.

*Loup Garou is a French word. You say it like
this: loo-ga-roo.

The Loup Garou would change into a wolf at night and eat all the food, and when the people chased him into the sea, he swam ashore in Acadia."

"And you think this Loup Garou is still here in Acadia?" asks Little Otter. "He would be dead by now!"

"Maybe it is the son that is here now. I am

not sure. But there *is* a Loup Garou here in
Acadia!"

The light in the forest is fading. An owl
hoots.

"If the Loup Garou is here," says Louis, "it is
time for him to change. Now!"

Little Otter tightens his bow, and bending low, looks through the trees.

"Your bow and arrows won't help us," Robert says. "You have to sprinkle salt on the Loup Garou's tail. Then he disappears. That is the only way to get the Loup Garou, my mother says. Nothing else can hurt him."

"I don't have any salt," Little Otter whispers.

"Neither do I," Louis says in a voice so low no one hears him. "It is very late!"

"I hear something!" Little Otter stands straight and still.

The boys listen. It is the farm bell ringing;

Robert's mother is calling him home.

"I am going home too." Little Otter starts to run. "May you be safe from the Loup Garou!" he calls back as he disappears into the woods toward the Micmac Indian camp.

"Good night, Robert," says Louis hurriedly. "I cannot hunt tomorrow. I am keeping the shop

for my father. He is going to a meeting, and *I* will be the blacksmith tomorrow!"

"Good night, Mr. Blacksmith! I hope no poor horse loses his shoe tomorrow."

Chapter II

Robert crosses the fields. He and his father have just cut the grass and it is drying, almost ready to store in the barn. The cattle need lots of hay for the long, cold winter. Robert and his father have harvested the wheat, too, for the crusty bread his mother bakes. Robert walks through the orchard, under the trees, heavy

with juicy apples almost ripe and ready to pick. Robert likes this work, but what he likes best is after harvest, before the snow and ice, when he and his father hunt and fish, while his mother makes jellies, soap, and candles and spins cloth. All that the family needs is made or grown on the farm, hunted from the woods, or fished out of the sea.

As Robert opens the cottage door, his mother
looks up from stuffing a quilt with goose
feathers. The new baby is asleep in his cradle
by the fire.

"Well Robert, have you brought me a partridge?"

"No. And we did not see the Loup Garou." Robert sits down on the wolf skin in front of the fire and rocks the cradle.

"That is because there is no such thing as the Loup Garou," says Robert's father, also coming in. He is short like Robert, wiry and strong. "That is just a story your mother told to pass the evening. But there are Englishmen, I can tell you, and they are worse than the Loup Garou. Better to hunt an Englishman!"

"Paul!" cries Robert's mother.

"It is true! The English want to take our land. Today, when I was in the village, there was a lot of talk. The English say they won the war long ago, and they say that this is Nova Scotia, not Acadia. The French must leave. This is *my* land, I say. Before me, it was my father's, and before him, his father's. Why should I leave?"

"Paul, you must be careful of what you say!"

"I will say what is true, Marie! Governor Lawrence has ordered all Frenchmen and French boys over ten years old to go to the church tomorrow. We will hear what the English king has to say. Robert, you are ten, and you must come with me."

"I will be there, Father! I will tell the governor what we think!"

Robert's mother gasps. "One outspoken Frenchman is enough for one family. Go with your father and *listen!*"

That night, lying in the loft under the thatched roof, Robert hears his mother whisper, "Paul, I am afraid. The English mean to do away with us!"

Chapter III

The next day finds Robert and his father with over four hundred other men and boys, all crowded into the village church. Louis is not there. Although he is taller than Robert, he will not be ten until next month. But Robert sees Louis' father and thinks: Louis will look like that someday, big, with black hair and great muscles in his arms.

The governor begins to read a paper in English. Someone translates it into French as he goes along: "In this year of our Lord, 1755, His Majesty, King George II. . . ." The paper says that the land and the cattle, all of it, belong to the English king! The Frenchmen are to be put on ships and sent away. No one knows where. Meanwhile, all are prisoners in the church! No one can leave, not even to tell the women what has happened. That will be done for them by the English soldiers, who are at this very moment in the French homes looking for guns.

The French men and boys are shouting and talking all at once. But no one can do anything, because the English slam the church door shut and throw the iron bolt across.

"I did not believe they would go this far. I must think of something!" Robert's father whispers to himself and Robert.

"I wish I were a grown man," Robert thinks, "instead of the smallest one here. I would—but what would I do?"

As the night goes on, the prisoners quiet down and try to sleep. They huddle together for warmth, but the stone floor is hard and cold and Robert and his father cannot sleep. Outside, they hear the guard's footsteps as he circles the church. Robert has just started to doze when his father whispers in his ear, "The

guard has stopped walking! Stand on my shoulders and see if you can reach the window."

Robert can just reach the window, a narrow slit made for a shaft of light. For once Robert is glad to be small.

"Go home! You are the man of the house now. Tell your mother not to worry about me. I will think of something."

Robert is halfway through the window. He is stuck! He hears the guard and manages to squeeze back out of sight. He waits, listening for the footsteps, and just as they crunch around the corner, he shoves himself all the way through the slit and drops to the ground.

Clouds drifting across the moon make racing shadows in the street. Robert runs like the shadows. He runs like Little Otter, swiftly and without noise, all the way home.

The English soldiers have been to his house. They have taken his father's gun and let the cows out of the field and scared the hens and pigs away. The English have told Robert's mother that the house belongs to the king now.

"The soldiers have burned the Landry's house! Ours may be next!" she cries. "And Paul is a prisoner! What can I do? I cannot leave the baby!"

"Don't worry, Mother! I will think of something. I can bring food and clothes to Father."

Robert's mother looks desperately around the room. "Here," she says, "bring him this cheese and bread."

"I will bring him the wolf skin, too, to lie on. The floor is so cold."

"But how can you get these things inside the church? You must not get caught!"

But Robert is already disappearing into the night. "Don't worry, Mother!" he calls back. "I will think of something."

The moon has left the sky when Robert gets to the church, and the guard is dozing by his fire in front of the door. Robert creeps around to the side and calls softly under the window, "Father! Mother has sent you food."

"Tie it to this." His father whispers back, lowering a rope made of his shirt, jacket, and pants tied together.

Instead, Robert climbs up and squeezes
through the window just as a rooster crows.

"Robert! You should not have come back!"

"I am going where you go, Father!" Robert
shivers and his father wraps him in the wolf
skin. Morning has come, but Robert is fast
asleep.

Chapter IV

Mothers, wives, and children are waiting outside the church when the English soldiers, bayonets fixed, throw open the church doors and begin to herd the men toward the ships that will carry them away.

"Father! Father!" Robert hears Louis' voice above all of the others. Louis' mother pulls at the coat of an English soldier. "Let us come, too," she begs. "How will Louis ever find his father again?"

The women crowd around, crying and calling, looking for their men. Children duck under the soldiers and run to their fathers. The soldiers are trying to hold back the women and children. Suddenly, the man in front of Robert

tries to knock a soldier down. Five soldiers are on the man in an instant. In the confusion, Robert's father drops on all fours with the wolf skin on his back. He looks like an animal!

"Run!" he hisses at Robert. "Run and I will chase you!" They are a good distance away

before a soldier turns and sees a wolf chasing a little boy. He fires at the wolf but a woman in the crowd jostles his arm, ruining his aim. He turns back to the prisoners. A soldier has all he can do to handle these wild women and their men; there is no time for one little boy about to be eaten by a wolf.

Around the corner, Robert's father stands up and laughs. "So, Robert! Now you have seen a real Loup Garou!"

"Father, you make a very good Loup Garou, and I tried to look frightened of you."

"Robert, you are too brave to look much like a frightened boy!"

When they reach home, Robert's mother hugs them until Robert's father says, "Marie, there will be time for that later if we move quickly now. We must hide. We will take only my hunting knife, the wolf skin and warm clothes. We will hide in the woods with our Indian friends."

They leave the house, closing the door behind them. At the end of the field, Robert looks back. He will not see his home again. Robert's mother looks back and Robert sees tears in her eyes, but she holds the baby tighter and walks on.

"Hurry!" says Robert's father. He does not look back.

Chapter V

In the woods, on their way to the Micmac camp, the family gathers berries to eat. Robert shows his father a beaver dam that he and Louis once saw and his father traps a beaver. They come at night to the Indian camp, where Little Otter's father makes them welcome and shares his meal of fresh deer meat.

Little Otter and Robert sit around the fire listening to stories the grown-ups tell. They are not as scary as the story of the Loup Garou. Robert's father talks of the English; Little Otter's father tells about Gluscap, the Great Spirit of the Micmac tribe.

"Gluscap once lived in Acadia. He planted seeds in the ground, and the Micmac people sprang from the seeds like trees and flowers do. Then, the white man came and Gluscap changed his dogs into rocks and his kettle into an island and moved his wigwam beyond the clouds."

"May the Micmacs never have to move their wigwam." Robert's father says softly.

The fire has burned low.

"Tomorrow, we will go hunting," says Little Otter. "I will bring salt in case we see the Loup Garou!"

"There is no such thing as the Loup Garou. We will hunt rabbits instead," Robert answers.

Inside Little Otter's birch bark wigwam, Robert lies on his wolf skin. He looks out at the stars and thinks of Louis. He moves closer to his father.

"There is a French colony in Louisiana," says his father, "where the great river meets the sea. It will not be easy, but we must find a way to get there."

In the woods a wolf howls. It is not a Loup Garou, but it is not an Englishman either. Robert snuggles into the wolf skin and falls asleep thinking. "Let the English have Nova Scotia; I have my family and we will find another Acadia."

Notes

The English forced the French out of Nova Scotia in just this way, and some of the French escaped and hid with the Micmac Indians, who had always been their friends. Many of the French Acadians finally came to southwest Louisiana, where their descendants, called Cajuns, live today. The Loup Garou is true! Well, almost. It is at least true that he existed in the stories told by the Acadians in Nova Scotia long ago, and in the stories told by the Cajuns of Louisiana today.